Christmas Day in the Morning

Christmas Day in the Morning

Text copyright © 1955 by Pearl Sydenstricker Buck (Mrs. Richard J. Walsh). Copyright renewed
1983 by Janice C. Walsh, Henriette C. Walsh, Mrs. Chieko Singer, Edgar Walsh, John W.
Walsh, Richard W. Walsh, Mrs. Jean C. Lippincott
and Carol Buck
Illustrations copyright © 2002 by Mark Buehner
Printed in the U.S.A. All rights reserved.
www.harperchildrens.com

Library of Congress Cataloging-in-Publication Data
Buck, Pearl S. (Pearl Sydenstricker), 1892–1973.
Christmas day in the morning / by Pearl S. Buck ; illustrated by Mark Buehner.
p.   cm.
Summary: A boy surprises his father on Christmas morning by getting up early and milking
the cows on their farm.
ISBN 0-688-16267-3 —— ISBN 0-688-16268-1 (lib. bdg.)
[1. Christmas——Fiction.   2. Farm life——Fiction.]   I. Buehner, Mark, ill.   II. Title.
PZ7.B879 Chh   2002   [E]——dc21   2001089497

1   2   3   4   5   6   7   8   9   10   ❖   First Edition

ON December 23, 1995, shortly after 2:00 A.M., my wife, Cara, woke me up because she had heard some strange noises and wanted me to investigate. Feeling pretty confident that there was no cause for concern, I got out of bed and sleepily descended the stairs. I was surprised and delighted by what I saw. My two children, Heidi, who was then ten, and Grant, who was seven, were busy cleaning the kitchen. Heidi warned me "not to tell Mom" because they wanted it to be a Christmas surprise. I went upstairs and told Cara that everything was fine.

When we woke the next morning, the main floor of the house had been cleaned. Grant had stayed awake, frequently checking the clock until about 2:00 A.M., when he woke up Heidi. They began to clean and did not stop for over two hours. There was little left for Cara and me to do for our family party that night, and though Heidi and Grant were both tired, I think they knew what a special gift of love they had given us.

Cara and I were touched and amazed by this sweet gift from our children, which was a response to their hearing "Christmas Day in the Morning" in church. It's been an honor for me to illustrate this wonderful and meaningful story that inspired my children to give my wife and me a Christmas gift we will always treasure.

Mark
Buehner

Christmas Day in the Morning

BY PEARL S. BUCK

ILLUSTRATED BY MARK BUEHNER

HARPERCOLLINS*PUBLISHERS*

☆

He waked suddenly and completely. It was four o'clock, the hour at which his father had always called him to get up and help with the milking. Strange how the habits of his youth clung to him still! Fifty years ago, and his father had been dead for thirty years, and yet he waked at four o'clock in the morning. He had trained himself to turn over and go to sleep, but this morning, because it was Christmas, he did not try to sleep.

☆

He slipped back in time, as he did so easily nowadays. He was fifteen years old and still on his father's farm. He loved his father. He had not known it until one day a few days before Christmas, when he overheard what his father was saying to his mother.

✫

"Mary, I hate to call Rob in the mornings. He's growing so fast, and he needs his sleep. If you could see how he sleeps when I go in to wake him up! I wish I could manage alone."

"Well, you can't, Adam." His mother's voice was brisk. "Besides, he isn't a child anymore. It's time he took his turn."

"Yes," his father said slowly. "But I sure do hate to wake him."

When he heard these words, something in him woke: his father loved him! He had never thought of it before, taking for granted the tie of their blood. Neither his father nor his mother talked about loving their children—they had no time for such things. There was always so much to do on a farm.

✫

✭

Now that he knew his father loved him, there would be no more loitering in the mornings and having to be called again. He got up after that, stumbling with sleep, and pulled on his clothes, his eyes tight shut, but he got up.

And then on the night before Christmas, that year when he was fifteen, he lay for a few minutes thinking about the next day. They were poor, and most of the excitement was in the turkey they had raised themselves and in the mince pies his mother made. His sisters sewed presents and his mother and father always bought something he needed, not only a warm jacket, maybe, but something more, such as a book. And he saved and bought them each something, too.

✭

☆

He wished, that Christmas he was fifteen, he had a better present for his father. As usual, he had gone to the ten-cent store and bought a tie. It had seemed nice enough until he lay thinking the night before Christmas, and then he wished that he had heard his father and mother talking in time for him to save for something better.

He lay on his side, his head supported by his elbow, and looked out of his attic window. The stars were bright, much brighter than he ever remembered seeing them, and one was so bright he wondered if it were really the star of Bethlehem.

"Dad," he had once asked when he was a little boy, "what is a stable?"

"It's just a barn," his father had replied, "like ours."

☆

Then Jesus had been born in a barn, and
to a barn the shepherds and the Wise Men
had come, bringing their Christmas gifts!
The thought stuck him like a silver dagger.
Why should he not give his father a special
gift, too, out there in the barn?

He could get up early, earlier than four o'clock, and he could creep into the barn and get all the milking done. He'd do it alone, milk and clean up, and then when his father went in to start the milking, he'd see it all done. And he would know who had done it.

At a quarter to three, he got up and put on his clothes. He crept downstairs, careful of the creaky boards, and let himself out. The big star hung lower over the barn roof, a reddish gold. The cows looked at him, sleepy and surprised.

☆

"So, boss," he whispered. They accepted him placidly, and he fetched some hay for each cow and then got the milking pail and the big milk cans.

☆

☆

He had never milked all alone before, but it seemed almost easy. He kept thinking about his father's surprise. His father would come in and call him, saying that he would get things started while Rob was getting dressed. He'd go to the barn, open the door, and then he'd go to get the two big empty milk cans. But they wouldn't be waiting or empty; they'd be standing in the milk house, filled.

☆

☆

The task went more easily than he had ever known it to before. Milking for once was not a chore. It was something else, a gift to his father who loved him. He finished, the two milk cans were full, and he covered them and closed the milk-house door carefully, making sure of the latch. He put the stool in its place by the door and hung up the clean milk pail. Then he went out of the barn and barred the door behind him.

☆

☆

Back in his room, he had only a minute to pull off his clothes in the darkness and jump into bed, for he heard his father up. He put the covers over his head to silence his quick breathing. The door opened.

"Rob!" his father called. "We have to get up, son, even if it is Christmas."

"Aw-right," he said sleepily.

"I'll go on out," his father said. "I'll get things started."

The door closed and he lay still, laughing to himself. In just a few minutes his father would know. His dancing heart was ready to jump from his body.

The minutes were endless——ten, fifteen, he did not know how many——and he heard his father's footsteps again. The door opened and he lay still.

"Rob!"

"Yes, Dad——"

His father was laughing, a queer, sobbing sort of a laugh. "Thought you'd fool me, did you?" His father was standing beside his bed, feeling for him, pulling away the cover.

"It's Christmas, Dad!"

☆

★

He found his father and clutched him in a great hug. He felt his father's arms go around him. It was dark, and they could not see each other's faces.

"Son, I thank you. Nobody ever did a nicer thing——"

"Oh, Dad, I want you to know——I do want to be good!" The words broke from him of their own will. He did not know what to say. His heart was bursting with love.

"Well, I reckon I can go back to bed and sleep," his father said after a moment. "No, hark——"

★

☆

"The little ones are waked up. Come to think of it, son, I've never seen you children when you first saw the Christmas tree. I was always in the barn. Come on!"

He got up and pulled on his clothes again, and they went down to the Christmas tree, and soon the sun was creeping up to where the star had been.

☆

☆

Oh, what a Christmas, and how his heart had nearly burst again with shyness and pride as his father told his mother and made the younger children listen about how he, Rob, had got up all by himself.

"The best Christmas gift I ever had, and I'll remember it, son, every year on Christmas morning, so long as I live."

They had both remembered it, and now that his father was dead he remembered it alone, that blessed Christmas dawn when, alone with the cows in the barn, he had made his first gift of true love.

☆